Universal Pictures and King World

PRESENT

THE LiTTLe RASCALS ™

THE NOVELIZATION

Adapted by Wendy Larson

From a screenplay written by
Paul Guay & Stephen Mazur
&
Penelope Spheeris

PRICE STERN SLOAN
Los Angeles

Designed by Beth Bender
© 1994 Universal City Studios, Inc. and Amblin Entertainment, Inc.
All rights reserved. The Little Rascals and The Little Rascals Characters are
trademarks of and copyrighted by King World Productions, Inc.
Licensed by MCA Publishing Rights, a Division of MCA, Inc.
Published by Price Stern Sloan, Inc.,
A member of The Putnam & Grosset Group, New York, New York.
Printed in the U.S.A. Published simultaneously in Canada.
ISBN 0-8431-3095-4
First Edition
1 3 5 7 9 10 8 6 4 2

Chapter 1

The He-Man Woman-Haters' Club

The Little Rascals' clubhouse was a special place. It was big and roomy, and it sat all by itself on a weed-filled lot. It had taken the Rascals a lot of work to get it just the way they wanted. But the best thing about the clubhouse was ... girls were never, ever allowed inside.

This afternoon, the Rascals were holding an emergency meeting of their club, the He-Man Woman-Haters. Spanky, the club's president, had sent out their dog Petey with the message. EMURGENCY MEETING. BE THERE OR DIE, read the note. From all over the town, boys stopped what they were doing and hurried to the club-house.

"You're okay ... you're okay ... you're okay ..." motioned Froggy, nodding to each kid as he entered the Rascals' clubhouse. Froggy paid close attention. He wanted to make sure no boy got inside unless he knew the special signal: hand under the chin, fingers wiggling. No outsiders were admitted. Buckwheat, Porky—Froggy let all of his friends in. But suddenly, Butch and Woim showed up!

Butch was the biggest bully in town. Woim was his side-kick. And now poor Froggy faced them alone.

"What's the sign?" Froggy asked, trying to sound tough.

"Here's my sign, Buster," yelled Butch. He shoved his fist in Froggy's face. Froggy took a step backward.

"You can't hit me!" he warned. "We're on club property!" Froggy was praying that Butch would go along with that one. Bullies weren't easy to persuade.

"He's right," Woim put in. "It's a No Slug Zone."

Butch shook his head, glaring at Froggy. "All right for now, yutz. But you better watch it!" He stalked off with Woim at his heels.

Whew. A close one. Froggy looked around to make sure there were no latecomers. Then he slipped inside the clubhouse and closed the door.

The clubhouse was filled with boys. Laughing and joking, they took their seats on wooden benches. Petey, the dog, and Elmer, the monkey, were there, too.

Stymie took charge. He picked up his gavel—really a can of beans tied to a stick—and smashed it down on the podium.

"Gentlemen and gentlemen, I give you our president, Spanky!" He drew back his arm with a flourish. The boys cheered as Spanky entered the clubhouse and made his way through the crowd.

"How are you?" Spanky asked one boy, shaking his hand. "Good to see you," he told another. "Your fly's undone," he whispered to a third.

Finally Spanky arrived at the podium. He took a deep breath. "Vice president Stymie, lead the men in the Pledge of Our Lesions."

"All raise your right hand," Stymie said in a serious voice. Everyone raised their left hand. "Your other right hand," Stymie said. Everyone changed hands.

"I, Stymie," declared Stymie.

"I, Stymie," repeated the boys.

Stymie rolled his eyes. "Member in good standing of the He-Man Woman-Haters' Club do solemnly swear to be a he-man and hate women, and not play with them, or talk to them unless I have to, and especially never fall in love, and if I do, may I die slowly and painfully and suffer for hours or until I scream bloody murder." He took a gulp of air.

The Rascals weren't too good at repeating things. But they tried. After they were through, Spanky began to speak.

"As you know, today I called an emergency meeting for a really important reason." Uh-Huh, one of the Rascals, was getting ready to write down what everybody said. "But first," said Spanky, looking around the room, "does anybody have any good stories?"

"Yeah," said Stymie. "This morning my sister left the toilet seat down!" Everyone booed.

"How rude!" cried Spanky. "Anyone else?"

"Yeah," said Froggy. "A girl moved in across the street from my house. And she came over to play with me!" The boys shouted with disgust. A girl was bad enough. But playing with a girl was even worse.

Froggy shook his head. "Don't worry. I got back at her."

"What did you do? What did you do?" chanted the Rascals.

"I whipped out my lizard," he announced proudly. He pulled out a lizard from his pocket.

"Good job, Frogman," Spanky told him. "As it says in our Declaration of Undependence ..."

"Irls-gay ink-stay!" yelled Stymie.

"And ow-hay!" put in Buckwheat.

"Are you gettin' this, Uh-Huh?" asked Spanky. He wanted to make sure everything was written down.

"Uh-huh," said Uh-Huh. But he hadn't written a thing.

"All right, men. Now, for today's business. The pride of

3

our club—the Blur!" Spanky pointed to a beautiful red go-cart that sat next to the podium. The Blur was deeply respected by the Rascals.

"The Blur's never been beaten since the beginning of time—five years ago!" Buckwheat said.

"There are guys who would kill to have a go-cart as perfect as The Blur," agreed Froggy.

"Well," said Spanky, leaning forward on the podium, "this Sunday is the Go-Cart Derby."

"This Sunday, we defend our honor, our undefeated streak, and our trophies," chimed in Stymie. The Rascals looked at each other with pride. The five trophies they had won sat on a special shelf in the clubhouse.

"Best of all, this year's trophy will be presented by none other than the famous Indy race-car driver, A. J. Ferguson!" Spanky said. He showed the Rascals a poster advertising the county fair.

"He's the best driver in the world!" said Stymie. The Rascals were very impressed.

"Can I hear an azuga?" asked Froggy.

"Azuga, azuga, azuga, azuga, azuga!" shouted the Rascals.

"Nice azugas," Spanky said approvingly. "And now, the reason for the emergency meeting. We have to choose a driver for The Blur."

Stymie took off his hat. Carefully, Spanky wrote the name of each Rascal on tiny pieces of paper, and dropped each piece into the hat. Stirring them up with his hand, he pulled one piece out.

Each Rascal closed his eyes and crossed his fingers. They all wanted to be chosen.

"Inspected by number seven!" Spanky declared, reading the words on the paper. The Rascals began to applaud, but then stopped. That was a number—not a Rascal!

"Sorry," apologized Spanky. He pulled out another piece of paper and grinned. "Men, our driver is none other than my lifelong chum, my best buddy in the whole world—the one, the only—Alfalfa!"

Cheers filled the clubhouse. Alfalfa was definitely the best choice. But where was he? His usual seat, the front bench in the clubhouse, was empty!

Chapter 2

Alfalfa in Love

Not far from the clubhouse, on a small rowboat in the canal, stood the he-est he-man of them all. The he-man with the big cowlick sticking up from his shiny black hair. Alfalfa. As he rowed, he was singing a love song. Alfalfa sang with all his heart. And who was he singing to? None other than the lovely Darla.

"You have the most beauteous voice I've ever heard," she said admiringly. She held a pretty umbrella over her head, shading her face from the sunlight.

"And I never took a lesson," Alfalfa said proudly. He gave Darla a big smile.

Meanwhile, the Rascals had left the clubhouse. They were looking for Alfalfa. They couldn't wait to tell him that he had been chosen to drive The Blur! Suddenly, the boys heard a funny noise—like a sick animal. And it was coming from the canal. With Spanky in the lead, the boys ran toward the sound.

Horrified, they watched as the rowboat floated their way.

"Alfalfa's with Darla!" cried Spanky.

"And she's a girl!" shouted Porky.

"This is the most terrible thing that's ever happened in the history of mankind," said Buckwheat sadly.

Alfalfa was oblivious to the horrified stares of the Rascals.

Darla blew him a kiss. He caught it. Opening his hand he released the kiss, and blew Darla another one. It was enough to make even Petey, the dog, sick.

"Oh, Darla, we are two hearts with but one beat, two brains with but one thought, two souls with but one shoe," said Alfalfa dramatically. Darla reached out and lovingly patted down his cowlick.

"It's worse than I thought," whispered Buckwheat.

"Hand me your fishin' pole!" Spanky said, grabbing Buckwheat's pole. "And somebody find some cans." The boys rigged up the cans and fishing pole—and soon they had a microphone. Carefully moving the pole over Darla's head, the Rascals listened.

"There is just one thing ..." Darla said to Alfalfa, batting her eyelashes, "sometimes I think you don't want to be seen with me."

"My darling dreamboat, don't be ridiculous!" Alfalfa protested. "I'm proud to be seen with you!"

"Then how can you belong to the Woman-Haters' Club?" pouted Darla. "I'm a woman. Sort of."

"Oh, I'm not like them. I'm sensitive. I'm into sharing, caring, feeling. I'm in touch with my feminine side," he said sweetly, staring into Darla's eyes.

Up on the bridge, the Rascals were furious with anger. How could Alfalfa say such things? How could he betray them?

Darla had wanted to ask Alfalfa something all day. Something important. She wanted him to be her singing partner in the county fair's talent show.

"You mean it?" asked Alfalfa. He was filled with happiness. "Let's have a picnic to celebrate."

"Okay. Why don't we have it at the clubhouse?" Darla suggested.

7

Alfalfa thought for a minute. That was out of the question. No girls were allowed in the clubhouse. But wait. Tomorrow was swimming day. No one would be around.

"Sure. Sounds good!" he told her.

* * *

"A picnic with a girl? In our clubhouse?!" cried Stymie when he heard the words through his can-and-fishing-pole microphone. What was the world coming to?

Spanky tried to come to his friend's defense. "That's not the Alfalfa I know. Darla has trapped him like a fly in her web of girl magic! If we can just make her hate him, he's free. It's up to us to save him," he told the Rascals.

They looked down at the rowboat. Was it too late?

Chapter 3

A Romantic Lunch

The Blur wasn't the only go-cart in the Go-Cart Derby. Butch and Woim were entering theirs, too. They called their cart The Beast.

"All right, Woim. Ready for the test run?" It was the next day. And Butch and Woim needed the practice. They were sitting in The Beast, which was at the top of a hilly street.

"Ready, Butch," said Woim. They pushed off. The cart picked up speed. It flew by houses and parked cars. But then it started to fall apart. A front fender. A left fender. A wheel.

"Aaaaaah!" they cried as they flew down the hill. With a crash, they came to a sudden stop—right in front of Alfalfa! He was on his way to visit Darla. He had told the Rascals he was home sick with a toothache.

"When's the last time we beat you up?" growled Butch, glaring at Alfalfa.

"Let's see," said Alfalfa nervously. He held a small bouquet of flowers in his hands. "Uh … yesterday?"

Butch got ready to throw a punch. Just then, Alfalfa cried out, "Look!" It was an old trick, but it worked. As Butch and Woim turned to look, Alfalfa took off. The bullies were fast, but Alfalfa was faster. He got away.

Butch was furious. "First chance we get, we steal The Blur!" he vowed angrily.

* * *

Darla and her friends were playing hopscotch outside Darla's house. They stopped their game when they saw Alfalfa approaching.

"I've come a-courtin'. These are for you," he said to Darla. From behind his back, he produced what was left of the bouquet. One bent flower and a bunch of stems.

"They're splendiferous," swooned Darla.

Grinning from ear to ear, Alfalfa closed his eyes and leaned in for a kiss. He wanted to be knocked off his feet. And he was—by a giant Doberman! *THUMP!* He landed hard on the ground. As Alfalfa rubbed his sore behind, he saw a fancy chauffeur-driven car pull up to the curb. The dog's owner got out of the car, and came strolling over to the kids. He was about Alfalfa's age. It was just a summer day—but the boy was dressed like he was attending a fancy party. He had a haughty smile on his face.

The boy clapped twice, and the dog ran to his side. Then the boy turned to Darla. "I hope Fifi didn't startle you. She's so playful."

Darla stared. This boy was very cute, she thought.

Alfalfa picked himself up off the ground. Who was this bozo? he thought.

"Allow me to introduce myself," the boy said grandly, staring into Darla's eyes. "My name is Waldo Aloysius Johnston the Third."

"And I'm Darla," she said sweetly.

"Excuse me," said Alfalfa indignantly. "I'm Alfalfa."

But Darla and Waldo weren't paying any attention to him. "We just moved into town. My father bought the oil

10

refinery," Waldo explained.

That was why he was so oily! thought Alfalfa.

"I hope to see you again soon," Waldo called out to Darla, as he got back into his car.

"I'll be in the county fair's talent show, if you want to see me," she replied.

Alfalfa was angry. Today was a big day. The day of his picnic for Darla. This was no time for fooling around with someone like Waldo! Grabbing Darla's arm, he led her to the clubhouse.

* * *

The table was set. The candles were lit. Everything was just right. Alfalfa helped Darla to her seat.

"I'm dazzled," she murmured. Darla had always wondered what the inside of the clubhouse looked like. Alfalfa had done a lovely job decorating it.

Alfalfa smiled. He sat down. *PFLOPP!* Somebody had stuck a whoopie cushion on his chair!

"Excuse me," he said, blushing. "I have a little fahrvergnugen."

Darla smiled demurely.

Outside the clubhouse, the Rascals giggled. They were watching through a peephole in the wall. Spanky held a list in his hand that read: "Things To Do." If things went as planned, Darla and Alfalfa would be finished for sure.

Alfalfa coughed nervously. He lit the candles, and started a tape in the tape deck.

"Grape soda?" he asked, holding up a bottle.

"Fill it to the brim, slim," Darla answered. Alfalfa filled two glasses with the purple drink. He and Darla were so busy looking at each other, they didn't notice the peephole—or the other hole that was in the wall. It was right next to the table. One of the Rascals reached his hand in, and quietly poured something into each glass.

"To us," toasted Darla. They each took a sip of the soda.

"Blechhh!!!!!" It tasted horrible! Outside the clubhouse, the Rascals jumped up and down. Happily, Spanky crossed off another item on his list.

Alfalfa didn't know what to think. He picked up the empty can of soda. "Must have been a bad year," he said, pretending to examine it.

Darla shrugged. "Here," she said, taking out a small bag. "I brought some sandwiches I made myself."

"Hey, me too," said Alfalfa, showing her his bag of sandwiches. "Say, why don't we swap? What's yours is mine, and what's mine is ours," he said sweetly.

Darla broke out into a smile. "You know just what to say to take a girl's breath away," she sighed. Darla handed her sandwich to Alfalfa, and took his.

As the two lovebirds looked at one another, a small shovel, full of sand, popped through the hole in the wall. It was Porky. Holding his hand steady, he emptied a pile of sand onto each sandwich.

Gulp. Alfalfa took a big bite. All this mushy stuff had made him pretty hungry. Darla took a big bite, too. She didn't care what kind of sandwich it was—all that mattered was that Alfalfa had made it

Alfalfa was having a hard time swallowing. This was one crunchy sandwich, he thought.

"You made a delicious sandwich," he said, mouthfull of sand.

With difficulty, Darla swallowed. "And so did you. Very crunchy," she croaked. Back outside, the Rascals were doubled over with laughter. Their plan was working perfectly.

12

"Porky, you sure know how to make a SAND-wich!" laughed Buckwheat.

Porky held up his hand. "That wasn't sand. That was kitty litter!"

"Ughhhh," said the Rascals. Disgusting! But Porky quickly reassured them that the kitty litter was fresh. That made everyone feel better.

Meanwhile, Alfalfa and Darla tried to eat their sandwiches. Alfalfa was anxious to finish. He had left the best for last. He handed Darla a Twinkie.

Darla looked the Twinkie over. It didn't smell bad. It didn't look sandy. Carefully, she bit into it—and her teeth hit something hard.

"Surprise!" cried Alfalfa as Darla spit a huge ring into her hand. "I had to eat six Cracker Jack® boxes to find it. It's a symbol of my undying affliction for you."

"It's beautiful," she told him. She put it on her finger. It fit perfectly. And it looked so pretty in the candlelight.

For a few moments, the two of them stared at each other. Alfalfa was making Darla nervous. She'd never had a candlelit dinner before. And nobody had ever given her a ring. Alfalfa looked a little uncomfortable too. What could he do to lighten things up?

He'd make her laugh. "I can do this," he said, wiggling his eyebrows. Then he wiggled his ears.

But Darla didn't laugh. "That's pretty good," she told him. "I can do this," she said. She stuck out her tongue— and touched her nose! Alfalfa smiled weakly.

Darla looked at Alfalfa. Her stomach felt fluttery. He wasn't embarrassed by her, she thought, her mind racing. He loved her! His friends weren't as important to him as she'd believed.

Alfalfa took a deep breath. The time was right. "Darla,

would you think me forward if I asked for a kiss?" Darla paused. Then she closed her eyes, and puckered her lips.

With joy in his heart, Alfalfa leaned forward. He pressed his lips to Darla's.

Chapter 4

Things Heat Up

"That's it!" fumed Spanky. He threw down his list in anger. "We've got to put an end to this right now!" Motioning to the Rascals, he headed straight for the club-house door. *BANG! BANG! BANG!* Spanky pounded with all his might.

With a jump, Alfalfa leaped in the air. He was caught! His heart beat fast and furiously. There was no time to lose. Quickly, he blew out the candles, and pushed the ironing board back into the wall. Yanking Darla up by her arm, he pushed her toward the closet.

"In my hurry to eat, I forgot to give you the tour!" he said hastily. "Here's our wall. Here's our other wall. And here's our closet!" Alfalfa tried to push Darla inside. She wouldn't go.

"Have you lost your mind?" she burst out. Darla liked to think of herself as a lady. She wasn't used to such treatment.

BANG! BANG! BANG! Alfalfa shot a worried glance at the door. "Uh … lost my mind? No! Misplaced, maybe, but not lost!" Again, he tried to push Darla into the closet.

Darla had had enough. She'd heard the banging, too. Alfalfa wasn't fooling her anymore.

"Just as I thought!" she told him, stamping her foot.

15

"You are ashamed of me!"

Alfalfa's head was spinning. "I'm not ... I'm not ashamed of you!" he told her. "I'm proud of you! I just don't want anybody to see you!"

Darla shook her head. "You ruined everything just so you could be number one on your pals' hit parade! Well, that does it, mister. I'm out of here!"

But before she could leave, Alfalfa sprang into action. Grabbing a napkin from the floor, he tied it around his head and jaw. Wasn't that what people with toothaches did? Alfalfa thought desperately. He opened the door and stepped outside.

"Hiya guys!" he said in what he hoped was a casual voice. "You're back early!" He kept his hand on the doorknob.

Inside the clubhouse, Darla was seething. Angrily, she pulled on the knob, but Alfalfa's grip was too strong. Glancing around the room, her eyes came to rest on something that could help her....

The Rascals glared at Alfalfa.

"How's the toothache?" demanded Spanky.

Alfalfa did some fast thinking. "Uh ... the dentist pulled my wisdom teeth," he answered, trying to look like he was in pain.

"Oh," said Spanky. Alfalfa began to feel relieved. Maybe this crazy story would work! "That explains why you're acting so stupid!" Spanky exclaimed.

Stymie stepped forward. "Well, we're going inside the clubhouse now," he told Alfalfa. The other Rascals waited to see what would happen.

"No, you're not!" Alfalfa replied. "Uh ... what I mean is, it's such a nice day outside! Nothin's goin' on in the clubhouse."

But something was going on. Something loud.

16

"Hey, what's that noise?" asked Stymie. *CRASH!* The Blur—with Darla driving—came smashing through the wall. Stunned, the Rascals watch as The Blur roared down the hill.

Stymie couldn't believe his eyes. As he turned back to face Alfalfa, his nose detected a strange smell. It was smoke! Wisps of smoke were wafting out of the clubhouse.

This was too much for Alfalfa. He stumbled backward from the doorway, clutching his stomach. White as a ghost, Alfalfa turned in the direction Darla had gone ... and fainted.

Spanky took charge. "Fire drill!" he shouted. "Let's get to work! Now!"

Stymie pointed to Buckwheat and Porky. "You two call the fire department!" The boys nodded. Then they sped off.

The other Rascals ran to a tool shed that was near the clubhouse and hurried inside. They were prepared for a situation like this. A small siren sat on top of the shed. Stymie grabbed its handle, and cranked it as fast as he could. "Wiroo, wiroo," squealed the siren.

A few seconds later, out came the Rascals. They wore fire fighters' gear from head to toe. They were ready.

Following Spanky's lead, they lined up and began to fill balloons with water.

"Fire!" Spanky yelled when the balloons were all filled. But no one threw a balloon. Instead, the boys looked at him with puzzled stares.

"We know it's a fire!" they all said together.

"No!" cried Spanky in exasperation. "I mean, shoot!" A slew of water balloons hit the side of the clubhouse. They didn't help much. So the Rascals ran to the apartment building nearby. There was a faucet there.

Forming a line, one boy filled a bucket with water and

passed it on to another, who spilled a little and passed it on to another, who spilled a little more and passed it on. When the bucket reached Froggy, who was last in line, all that was left were a few drops. In desperation, Froggy took a deep breath and tried to blow the fire out.

Meanwhile, Buckwheat and Porky weren't having much luck calling for help. They had found a phone booth. But there were three people ahead of them. And they didn't dare cut the line, fire or no fire. Finally, they got to the front.

"Quick," Porky asked, "what's the number for 911?"

Buckwheat stared at his friend. "How do I know?" he said, panicking. The two boys looked at each other. Their shoulders drooping, they headed back to the burning clubhouse.

The Rascals continued to fight the fire. But things were looking grim. Stymie and Uh-Huh found a hose. Spanky was waiting.

"Okay, let her rip!" Spanky shouted. That was all Uh-Huh needed to hear. With all his strength, he turned the water on.

Spanky waited. Why wasn't the water coming? Just as he was ready to yell again, water came shooting out of the hose. The pressure was so strong that the hose jumped straight into the air—and Spanky went with it! Somehow, he managed to point the water at the clubhouse.

It worked. The flames died down. The fire was out. Gently, Uh-Huh turned off the water, and Spanky's hose lowered to the ground. The Rascals stared at the clubhouse—or what was left of it. All their hard work was destroyed. And who was to blame?

Only one person. And he was still lying on the grass. Buckwheat and Porky grabbed two water balloons, and dropped them on Alfalfa's head.

18

"Hey ... wha—" sputtered Alfalfa, sitting up with a jolt. "Darla!" he yelled, struggling up and running toward her. Darla had returned to view the wreckage. BAM! Darla threw out her arm, and punched Alfalfa smack in the face.

"I'm never going to speak to you as long as I live!" she cried, as Alfalfa fell to the ground. Darla took off the ring Alfalfa had given her and threw it. As she turned to go, Waldo arrived.

"Darla, Darla, Darla," he said soothingly. "May I offer you a ride in my father's car—and a dip in my father's swimming pool?" he asked, offering her his arm.

Darla smiled. She'd had enough of Alfalfa and his little games. With a toss of her head, she took Waldo's arm, and headed for the car.

Alfalfa watched them go. And then he turned to face his friends.

Chapter 5

Law and Order

The clubhouse was in ashes. The smell of burning wood and smoke filled the air. Slowly, the Rascals formed a circle around Alfalfa.

"Now we have no place to go to get away from grown-ups," Stymie said, his voice cracking.

"Our lives are over," exclaimed Porky.

"And it's all your fault!" accused Spanky. He glared down at Alfalfa. There was only one thing they could do....

*   *   *

"Order in the court! Order in the court! Send in the prisoner!" said Spanky in a loud voice. He was wearing his judge uniform—his father's black bathrobe. All of the Rascals were assembled in what was left of the clubhouse. They were holding a special meeting ... a meeting to decide the fate of Alfalfa.

 With Buckwheat on one side and Porky on the other, Alfalfa slowly marched to the front of the clubhouse. Buckwheat and Porky each held fishing pole "guns" in their arms.

Froggy cleared his throat. "People versus Alfalfa Switzer, criminal case number one," he announced.

Spanky nodded at Stymie to begin.

"Alfalfa," said Stymie, "you are accused of burning down our clubhouse. You violated the number one—and only—

rule of the He-Man Woman-Haters' Club," he said. He paused for a moment as Spanky pulled out the club's rule book. It was a bit burned, but Spanky could still read the words.

"NO GIRLS ALLOWED!" shouted Spanky, slamming the book shut. "Now, how do you plead?"

Alfalfa fell to his knees. He begged his friends for mercy. He hadn't meant to burn down the clubhouse. It was an accident. Wouldn't they give him another chance?

Spanky listened carefully to what Alfalfa had to say. Then, he spoke. "In keeping with club policy, we will give you a fair and impartial trial before we convict you," he told Alfalfa.

"But I don't even have a lawyer," objected Alfalfa.

"Yes you do," replied Spanky. He pointed to Porky, the youngest Rascal. Porky gave Alfalfa a big grin. Alfalfa shuddered. With Porky for a lawyer, he might as well give up.

Just like in a real courtroom, each side got to call in witnesses. The first witness was Buckwheat.

"Repeat after me," said Froggy. "I solemnly swear to tell the truth, the whole truth, and … what's the rest of it?"

"I solemnly swear to tell the truth, the whole truth, and what's the rest of it?" Buckwheat recited.

Froggy shook his head. "You may take the witness stand," he told him. But Buckwheat didn't move.

"You may take the witness stand," repeated Buckwheat.

"No, you don't have to repeat what I say anymore," Froggy said, annoyed.

"No, you don't have to repeat what I say anymore," Buckwheat said cheerfully.

"Knock it off!" yelled Froggy.

"Knock it off!" Buckwheat yelled back. Finally Spanky cut in. He told everyone to take their seats. Then Stymie asked his first question.

"What happened?" he demanded.

Buckwheat stood up and pointed at Alfalfa. "He did it! He did it!"

Spanky and Stymie smiled with satisfaction. With a worried glance, Alfalfa looked over at his lawyer, Porky. Surely Porky would have some questions to ask, too. But no. Porky didn't have one thing to say.

One by one, each Rascal got on the witness stand. And each one pointed a finger at Alfalfa. Petey lifted up an accusing paw. Even Porky got caught up in the excitement—and turned against his client.

"The prisoner will rise for sentencing," announced Spanky, banging his gavel. Alfalfa stood up slowly. "Would you like to make a statement?"

Alfalfa swallowed. "Just that ... just that ... I never knew liking a girl could lead to all this," he confessed. "I let my pals down. I let the club down. I even let my best friend down," he said, looking over at Spanky.

Spanky saw how hard it was for Alfalfa to say what he'd said. He even felt a little sorry for him. But that still didn't erase what had happened.

"Alfalfa Switzer," he said in a deep voice, "I hereby sentence you to execution at dawn."

Stymie put up his hand. "Your honor, may I suggest since he was trapped like a fly in a woman's web of lies, he be put on probation. While on probation, he alone will be responsible for guarding the go-cart ... day and night."

Murmuring their approvals, the Rascals nodded. This was a good punishment. They might be he-men, braver than brave—but spending the night outside in the dark was something everybody was afraid of.

"And," finished Stymie, "you may never again talk to, see, or even think about Darla, or else."

22

Chapter 6

Water and Wood

Far above the crashing waves of the ocean, on a wild, rocky cliff, stood two lone figures. Alfalfa and Darla.

"Darla, Darla, Darla!" cried Alfalfa. He was dressed in a kilt. Arms outstretched, he ran toward his sweetheart.

"Alfalfa, Alfalfa, Alfalfa!" cried Darla, throwing her arms around him. Wildly, they spun each other about.

"My lady, I'll never leave you," Alfalfa told her. "Except right now. I'm off to join Sir Spankus." He pointed behind Darla, where Spanky and the rest of the gang stood. They were holding lanterns, and they, too, wore kilts.

"But where will you go?" wailed Darla. "What will you do?"

Alfalfa looked down at Darla. "War and plundering, violence and pillaging, scratching and spitting. The usual. Farewell, my sweet petunia!"

"You must choose between us. Maybe this will help make up your mind," said Darla, planting a big kiss on Alfalfa's lips. Just as her mouth touched his, a flash of lightning shot across the sky. The Rascals, lanterns raised, moved toward them. Elmer, the monkey, began to beat on his drum.

"Traitor! We must slay you before your forbidden love destroys us!" Spanky said fiercely. The Rascals were getting closer.

Panicking, Alfalfa turned to Darla. Oh! She was angry, too! Alfalfa was so scared that his cowlick turned white. Stumbling backward, he watched in terror as his former friends pressed in on him.

"Choose or die! Choose or die! Choose or die!" they chanted. Alfalfa looked down below. He was at the edge of the cliff. With a scream, he fell over ... and belly flopped into the powerful surf of the ocean. . . .

Pitter-pat. Pitter-pat. Alfalfa sat up in alarm. His heart beat fiercely. But he was alive! He looked at his arms and legs. There didn't seem to be any broken bones. But wait. He wasn't in the ocean. Now he remembered. He was in a tent—guarding The Blur. And there in front of him stood Spanky, Stymie, Froggy, Uh-Huh, Buckwheat, Porky, and Petey.

"We came to keep you company," Buckwheat said.

Alfalfa gave them a little smile. Then he realized something. "Why am I soaking wet?" he asked, confused.

"Don't worry, Alfalfa," Porky whispered loudly. "I used to have the same problem."

"Relax," said Spanky. "It's just a hole in the tent." To prove his point, Spanky gave the side a poke. A flood of water washed over Alfalfa.

* * *

While the Rascals were on their rainy camp-out, Darla and her girlfriends were having a nice indoor slumber party.

"Why are boys such jerks?" Darla asked, taking a swig of cola.

"I heard it's all a matter of generics," said her friend Mary Ann. The other girls nodded. They'd all heard the same

24

thing.

Sighing, Darla took another sip of cola. "But then, sometimes boys can be so ooo-la-la," she said.

"Yeah. . . ." swooned the girls.

Mary Ann gave Darla a sharp look. "You're *not* thinking about Alfalfa, are you?"

Darla shook her head. "Oh, no. No, no, no." With a faraway glance in her eyes, she reached for a cheese puff.

* * *

At that very moment, Alfalfa was shaking his head, too. "Oh, no, no. I'm not thinking about Darla," he told his friends.

"Good!" said Spanky emphatically.

Froggy nodded his head in agreement. "Babes are like a bad song. Once you get 'em stuck in your head, you can't get 'em out again."

The next morning, Spanky went to the local lumberyard. "Howdy, mister," he said to the sales clerk. "Me and my buddies have to build a new clubhouse."

"We need to buy some lumber," added Stymie. Behind him stood the rest of the Rascals. They had brought empty wagons along to help cart back the wood.

Spanky emptied out his pocket onto the counter. Coins, bottle caps, buttons—all sorts of things spilled out.

"Give us all the wood you can for this much, please," he asked. The Rascals waited expectantly.

The sales clerk reached under the counter, and came up with a small piece of wood. He laid it on the counter. The Rascals couldn't believe it. That was it? One lousy little piece of wood?

The Rascals told the salesclerk about the clubhouse. And they told him how much wood they had hoped to buy. The salesclerk shook his head. All that wood would cost $450.00!

With their empty wagons dragging behind them, the

boys left the store.

"Four hundred and fifty dollars for lumber?" Stymie said sadly.

"Where can we get that kind of moola?" Spanky asked him.

Stymie shrugged. "I don't know. But you know what they say. Wood doesn't grow on trees." As the boys walked down the street, they noticed a sign in a bank window. INSTANT LOANS, it read.

The Rascals stopped in their tracks. Spanky gathered everyone around. "All in favor say 'yoy yoy yoy yoy yoy.' "

"Yoy yoy yoy yoy yoy," they chorused.

"The yoys have it. Stymie, Froggy, you two come with me. This will be easy as one-two-three," Spanky told them.

But it wasn't. Mr. Welling, the loan officer, would not even speak with them. Stymie and Froggy were mad. They didn't like to be treated like kids. But just because they didn't get in this time didn't matter, thought Spanky. He had an idea.

Later that day, two very tall men, dressed in long coats and black hats, entered the bank. Were these heros? Villains? No—it was none other than Spanky and Stymie, standing on the shoulders of other Rascals. The coats covered them up. Both boys wore fake white beards. The disguise was perfect.

Mr. Welling was hard at work. Spanky spoke first.

"Hello, my good man," he said in a deep voice.

"Gentlemen, won't you sit down," Mr. Welling said. He had not taken his eyes off his desk.

Spanky and Stymie looked at each other. They couldn't sit down. "We can't sit down, my good man," Spanky informed him. "The point is, we want to take out a big loan."

"Of course," said Mr. Welling pleasantly. "What is your

account number?"

"Uh ... seven?" guessed Spanky.

Mr. Welling looked up. Seven was not an account number. Glaring at the two "men," he realized he'd been tricked. Getting up, he yanked the beards off both boys.

"I've heard enough. If you were my kids, I'd punish you," he told them sternly.

"If we were your kids, we'd punish ourselves!" Stymie said.

"Get outta here!" said Mr. Welling, his voice rising in anger. Realizing they weren't going to get any money, the boys left.

Chapter 7

Alfalfa Writes a Note

Back at the clubhouse—or what was left of the club-house—the rest of the Rascals sat and waited for their friends to come back from the lumberyard.

"She loves me ... she loves me not ... she loves me!" Alfalfa declared, pulling the last petal off a flower. "It's true! She really does care!" He pointed an accusing finger at Buckwheat and Porky. "You guys don't know what you're talkin' about."

Buckwheat and Porky looked at each other. It had taken Alfalfa hours to come up with the answer he wanted. A pile of petal-less flowers laid beside them.

"I have to see her," Alfalfa told his friends. Even if it did violate his probation. Even if he wasn't supposed to leave his post.

Suddenly, Alfalfa snapped his fingers. "I know! I'll write Darla a message. And you two can take it to her."

Porky looked uncomfortable. "Wait a second. We're he-man woman-haters. We can't deliver love notes."

Alfalfa tried to look surprised. "Love notes? No! This is a *hate* note."

This sounded much better. "A hate note?" asked Buckwheat. "Okay."

Alfalfa began to write his note. It read: "Dear Darla, I can't live without you ... really ... I'm not kidding. Your Romeo, Alfalfa."

But Alfalfa didn't tell Buckwheat and Porky what was *really* on the note. He told them something very different.

"Dear Darla," started out Alfalfa. "I hate your stinking guts. You make me vomit," he said, his voice getting louder. "You are scum between my toes. Love, Alfalfa."

Alfalfa looked at his two friends. They believed every word he'd said! Carefully, Alfalfa signed his name on the note. There! It was perfect. Darla would get her message. And the Rascals would still believe he was a he-man. He handed the note to Porky, and watched as the two boys headed down the street.

*   *   *

"Bringggg," rang the doorbell. Porky and Buckwheat were outside Darla's house.

"Yes?" asked Darla. She and Mary Ann had been practicing some ballet steps for their recital later that day. They didn't want to be interrupted.

Porky shifted his feet nervously. "Buckwheat, where's the note?"

"I know I got it here somewhere," answered Buckwheat. He began emptying his pockets. Bubble gum, rocks, pennies ... everything but the note.

Porky sniffled. He blew his nose. "We'll find that note," he told Darla between blows. She tapped her foot impatiently.

All of a sudden, Buckwheat turned to Porky. "I know. I gave it to you!" he said.

Porky looked down at his tissue. But it wasn't a tissue. It was the note!! Hastily, he shoved the note back in his pocket and shot a worried glance at Buckwheat.

"It's okay," said Buckwheat, catching on. "I remember what the note said. 'Dear Darla, I hate your stinking guts. You make me vomit. You are scum between my toes. Love, Alfalfa.' " There! He'd done it word for word. He and Porky smiled proudly at Darla and Mary Ann.

Alfalfa felt sick when Buckwheat and Porky returned and told him what they had done. Sure, that's what he'd *told* them the note had said. But those were lies. The note had really said *nice* things.

"Was she upset?" he asked worriedly.

Buckwheat and Porky looked at each other. Darla had seemed pretty mad. And Mary Ann had gasped a lot. They nodded their heads at Alfalfa.

Things were not working out like he'd planned, thought Alfalfa. He'd have to go see her in person. So what if Spanky had said he couldn't speak with Darla. Spanky wasn't his boss! He could do whatever he felt like. He turned to leave … and ran straight into Spanky.

Spanky agreed that Alfalfa should see Darla. Not to apologize. To break things off completely.

Chapter 8

Ballerinas?

"Trust me, this is for your own good," Spanky assured him. The two boys were heading up the steps of the dance hall where Darla's recital was going to be.

"Don't you have any pride?" asked Spanky. "Isn't it enough that she slugged you silly, threw your Cracker Jack® ring in the dirt, and mortifried you in front of your pals?"

Alfalfa thought for a minute. "Is this a trick question?" he asked. Then, they found themselves at the door. Ms. Roberts, the ballet teacher, was there.

"Hello," she said to one family. She smiled down at Spanky and Alfalfa. "Yes, little boys?" she said.

"Excuse me, ma'am. We need to talk to Darla," Spanky said.

Ms. Roberts was firm. No one could see the dancers. They needed to practice. That was all Alfalfa needed to hear. He did not want to see Darla now anyway! But Spanky had other plans. Grabbing Alfalfa's hand, he motioned to the steps. They would sit and wait. Spanky took a frog out of his pocket and handed it to Alfalfa. Maybe that would cheer him up.

Back at the clubhouse, Buckwheat and Porky were on

duty. Marching back and forth with their fishing poles, they guarded The Blur. But they weren't alone.

"This'll be like stealing candy from a baby!" said a low voice. Butch! He and Woim were hiding out in some bushes near the clubhouse. They were going to try to steal The Blur.

Left. Left. Left, right, left. Buckwheat and Porky kept marching.

"Hey," cried Porky. A duck was walking a few yards in front of them. Tied to the duck's leg was a long string … with a dollar bill stuck on it! Dropping their poles, the two Rascals ran after the duck.

No matter how fast they ran, they couldn't catch it. Each time they got closer, the duck moved faster. Buckwheat and Porky didn't give up. They'd catch that duck for sure!

Butch and Woim grinned evilly. Now that those two were out of the way, The Blur would be theirs.

"The racer is ours," said Butch, stepping in front of The Blur. But the Rascals were prepared for something like this. They had rigged up a booby trap. The keys to the racer were tied to a string—which was attached to a rope—on which hung a heavy boot—which would smash into a bench—and knock over a big bucket of pickles!

Butch grabbed the keys. *WHOOSH! SMASH!* A startled Butch and Woim looked left and right and then up. Too late. Pickles and pickle juice—poured over their horrified faces.

Meanwhile, Buckwheat and Porky had caught up with the duck. And they had gotten the dollar bill, too.

"Nothin' like a security system to give you peace of mind," Buckwheat said contentedly.

With the smell of pickles all over them, Butch and Woim headed for home. As they walked by the dance hall, Butch spotted Alfalfa and Spanky. He'd make them pay for this!

"Aaaah!" cried Alfalfa when he saw the two bullies running toward them. He and Spanky tore into the dance hall.

They needed to find disguises. And quick. Frantically, the boys ran into the costume room. Tutus, wigs, and leotards spilled out. Alfalfa looked at Spanky. Spanky looked at Alfalfa. They didn't have any choice.

Butch and Woim were hot on their trail. The bullies raced down the hallway, and pushed open the first door they saw. *AHH!* A bunch of girls screamed. Wrong door. Butch and Woim ran back down the hallway. They opened another door. *OH!* More screams. Next they came to the costume room. The door to the room swung open.

"Hiya, fellas," said a high-pitched voice. It was Spanky, dressed in a ballerina outfit. He gave Butch and Woim a quick smile, and pulled Alfalfa—who was also in a tutu and wig—into the hallway.

"Say, you two chicklets see a couple of ugly mugs who ran in here?" Butch called after them.

"You mean besides you?" asked Alfalfa sweetly. Spanky pinched him. "I think they went in there," he said, pointing to Ms. Roberts door.

"Whew," said Spanky. They watched Butch and Woim walk in on Ms. Roberts. She angrily ushered the bullies out the door. "Let's ange-chay and amscray!" Spanky blurted out.

"You took the words right out of my mouth," said Alfalfa gratefully. He pushed the exit door.

"Hi!" said a cheery voice. Darla! This wasn't the exit. It was the girls' changing room. And there was Mary Ann and all of Darla's other friends, too. Spanky and Alfalfa's eyes grew wide.

"Are you a Sugar Plum fairy?" asked a girl, pointing to their tutus.

Alfalfa nodded. Sweat beads were beginning to form on his forehead. And the frog! He had been holding the frog in his hand all this time.

"Pardon me," he said in a girlish voice. "I'm sweating like a pig. It's the recital."

Darla gave Alfalfa her handkerchief. He wiped the sweat off his forehead. And then he scrubbed underneath his arms. After he finished, he offered the handkerchief back to Darla.

She motioned for him to keep it. "I'm excited too," Darla told him. "My boyfriend Waldo is going to be here."

Mary Ann smiled knowingly. "He's driving her to his mansion for tea."

"Do you have any boyfriends?" asked Darla.

"No!" shouted the boys. "But," said Alfalfa, pausing. "There is one boy I'd love to get to know. His name is Alfalfa." Spanky gave him a dirty look.

"*I* used to know an Alfalfa," said Darla, surprised. "He took the best years of my life!"

"Same here," said Spanky.

"I don't miss him at all," Darla said with a sigh. "Except … his voice. When he sings he makes me melt like a popsicle on the Fourth of July!"

Suddenly, the kids were interrupted by Ms. Roberts. It was showtime. The girls headed out to take their places.

Chapter 9

Tutu Trouble

The dance hall was crowded. Lots of parents and friends had come. Waldo was there, too. Against their better judgment, Alfalfa and Spanky were forced to join hands with the girls, and danced out onto the stage.

In a panic, Alfalfa tossed the frog to Spanky. Spanky didn't want the frog either. Where could he put it? Quickly, he shoved it down Alfalfa's leotard.

Spinning and twirling, the girls began to dance. Alfalfa and Spanky tried to keep up, but it was hopeless. The frog was too distracting for Alfalfa. Leaping and jumping, he danced like a madman around the stage, hoping the frog would jump out of the leotard. The girls stopped dancing—they couldn't take their eyes off the crazy ballerina.

Finally, the music ended. Everyone, including Alfalfa, took a bow. The audience was confused, but clapped anyway. Ms. Roberts was furious. She couldn't wait to get her hands on Alfalfa. But before she could, he and Spanky were offstage and headed out the door.

"Good thing I finally caught that frog," said Alfalfa.

"Yeah. Now all you have to worry about is warts!" laughed Spanky.

Warts? Ugh! Alfalfa began to tear off his clothes. So what if he was now in his underwear? He didn't want to have warts. With a ribbit of relief, the frog leaped from Alfalfa's leotard, and onto the ground.

Just then, Ms. Roberts hurried out into the hallway. Her face was as red as a tomato. "You've ruined my recital, you ragamuffin!" she shrieked, running toward Alfalfa. The two Rascals spun around and raced for the door. Then they came to a halt. They had spotted Butch and Woim waiting for them.

"I'll distract them while you make a getaway," Spanky said quickly. Spanky was still in his costume. He could still fool them into thinking he was a girl.

"Thanks, Spanky. You sure are a pal," Alfalfa whispered. If the two bullies saw him in his underwear, he'd never live long enough to live it down.

"Hello, again," murmured Spanky.

Butch and Woim were taken by surprise. They had fallen under the husky ballerina's spell. As they stared at Spanky, Alfalfa slipped away from the dance hall and made his escape.

Walking like a fancy movie star, Spanky headed in the same direction Alfalfa had. The only problem was, he didn't see a big tree branch that hung over his head. Spanky's wig got caught on it—and his disguise was destroyed!

With cries of anger, Butch and Woim started after Spanky. They lost him. But they found somebody else. Alfalfa!

Alfalfa had been trying to sneak quietly down the street. He didn't think things could be much worse. He'd made a fool of himself at the recital in front of Darla and Waldo. And now, here he was, walking down the street in his underwear.

With a gasp, he saw Butch and Woim.

"Nice tan," Butch sneered. "Any last words?"

Alfalfa thought for a moment. "See ya!" he yelled, running across the street.

Alfalfa ran as fast as he could. Zigzagging through yards, running down sidewalks—anything to get away. In front of him stood a giant mansion. This was as good a place as any, thought Alfalfa. Tearing up the walk, he squeezed past a woman in the doorway. In her hands were two large cakes.

He was just in time. The woman shut the door—right in Butch and Woim's faces.

Poor Alfalfa. Now that he was in, he didn't know how to get out. He hurried past a startled maid, and out the back door.

"GRRRR!" snarled a Doberman. It was Waldo's dog, Fifi! And if that was Waldo's dog, then this must be Waldo's house! But Alfalfa didn't want to think about that now. He had to get away from Fifi!

With a splash, Alfalfa jumped into the pool. He kicked up a storm. There. All that splashing should scare off the dog. As Fifi stood and stared into one end of the pool, Alfalfa pulled himself out of the other and began to run again.

Hmmmm, thought Alfalfa. What a breezy day this was. He felt so free, so alive, so … so … naked! He was naked! In horror, he looked back toward the pool. His underwear was floating gently on the water. Running back, Alfalfa bent over to retrieve it. But not before Darla and Waldo saw him.

Could anything more embarrassing happen? Alfalfa thought to himself. "Darla," he said, "there's a perfectly logical explanation"— his eyes darted to the growling Fifi—"which I'll make up later!" Underwear in hand, Alfalfa took off.

Chapter 10

Spanky's Big Plan

Soon it was time for the county fair. A petting zoo was set up with baby animals. Quilts and crafts were for sale. A ferris wheel twirled in the sky. The smell of french fries and burgers drifted through the air.

The Rascals all took deep breaths. They had come to the fair with a plan. A plan to make enough money to rebuild the burned-down clubhouse. There were lots of people at the fair. And these people had money.

Each Rascal pitched in, and soon they had set up their own booth. They had used shower curtains and mop handles to make it. Spanky finished adjusting a curtain.

"Spanky, me and Porky got an idea," Buckwheat said, tugging on Spanky's shirt.

Spanky didn't want to listen. What did they know? They were just kids. He hung up one of the signs they'd made. It read: SPANKY'S BELIEVE IT OR ELSE—ONE KWARTER. A few passersby stopped to read it. In a flash, Spanky began twirling a cane.

"Ladies and gentlemen," he said, motioning to the people, "enter if you dare!" A few people stopped.

"See the freaks of nature, gathered from the five incontinents of the Earth!" bellowed Stymie. He grinned as a few more people gathered around.

One man stepped forward. He handed Spanky a quarter, and entered. And then a few more people stepped forward. They, too, each gave Spanky a quarter and entered the booth.

Stymie began to rap. "A thing that's so appealing, you gotta pay to see it. And when you feast your peepers, you'd rather see than be it." He took a breath. "It knows all, it sees all—ask it any question. A human head without a tummy, it gets no indigestion."

Slowly, a curtain opened to reveal a small table with a long tablecloth on it. In the middle was Uh-Huh's head. Everyone oohed and aahed. Until a buzzing fly landed on Uh-Huh's nose. Swat! Uh-Huh took his hand out from under the table and hit the fly. A ripple of disappointment went through the crowd.

Spanky tried to take charge. "Step right up and let the Fantastical Froggini guess your most recent meal," he declared. Froggy sat in a booth, a very serious expression on his face.

"Broccoli?" he guessed, as the first contestant came up and breathed in his face.

The crowd thinned out a little. Spanky and Stymie could see that they were losing interest, but they were determined to keep trying.

Spanky motioned to an old woman. "Step right up and witness Wheezer the Wonder Boy burp The Battle Hymn of the Republic!"

Wheezer musically burped as best he could.

"He missed a verse," the old woman complained to Stymie. Reluctantly, he handed the old woman back her quarter.

Stymie tried another rap. "A sight that's so revolting, you'll wish that you were blind. A vision so disgusting, you think you lost your mind! Truth is stranger by a mile than any made-up fiction. So step right up and see the Weird Four-Foot Man Eating Chicken!"

Once again, Froggy sat in the booth. This time he had a fake moustache on. Bite after bite, he devoured a big plate of fried chicken.

With hope in his eyes, Stymie looked at the crowd. Not many people were left. He turned to Spanky, throwing up his hands in defeat.

"Hey, you!" Spanky called out to the last customer. "Rub a fat kid's head for luck?" The man shook his head in disgust and stormed out the door.

All of the Rascals were at the fair, except for Alfalfa. He was alone at the clubhouse, trying not to think of Darla. "I will not think of Darla. I will not think of Darla," he wrote sadly, over and over again.

Petey sat by his side. "Maybe Spanky's right," Alfalfa said. "Maybe I should just forget about love. All it's ever gotten me is a punch in the face, a frog in my leotard, a naked chase, and a bad lunch."

He put down his pencil. He was out of paper. Petey ran to get some.

"No, not that kind of paper!" Alfalfa said, pointing to the roll of toilet paper Petey had in his mouth. Petey trotted back out, and returned with a regular sheet of paper.

"Thanks, Petey," Alfalfa said. He began to write, but noticed that the paper had already been written on. It was Spanky's sabotage checklist!

He'd been tricked by that sleazy Spanky! It was Spanky's fault that Darla hated him. Alfalfa just hoped that it wasn't too late to win her back.

With determination in his heart, Alfalfa started up The Blur. Petey jumped in beside him, and they sped off.

Chapter 11

The Barber of Seville

"C'mon Spanky. So things didn't quite pan out," Stymie told his friend. He was trying his best to console him. But Spanky didn't want to hear it.

"Didn't quite pan out?! We have less money now than when we came!" he yelled.

The Rascals trudged past vegetable stands and cotton candy vendors. Soon they came upon a talent show tent. Sitting outside the tent were Buckwheat and Porky. A sign was propped up next to them. ADMISHUN $3, it read.

"Three dollars, please," said Porky as a woman came up to the tent. She took out the money and handed it over. Behind her were more people. Every one of them had dollar bills in their hands.

Spanky couldn't believe his eyes. "What's going on?" he asked Buckwheat.

"We just put up this sign and people started paying us," Buckwheat told him, showing him the wad of money he had.

"There must be hundreds of enchiladas here! Buckwheat, Porky—you're geniuses!" Stymie exclaimed, leaping joyously into the air.

Spanky motioned for Buckwheat and Porky to get up.

He wanted to collect the money. He liked being in charge. With a smile on his face, he took his seat behind a table.

At that moment, Miss Crabtree, the Rascals' school-teacher, came around the corner. She read the sign, and gave a puzzled look to the boys.

Even though she was a woman, the Rascals couldn't help but like her. She was just too pretty. "Miss Crabtree!" they said in unison.

But Miss Crabtree was angry. And the boys knew it. So the Rascals ran and hid inside the talent show tent. That is, everyone but Spanky.

"Spanky McFarland!" scolded Miss Crabtree. "I'd expect this from a four-year-old, but not from you!" She took the money from Spanky's hand, and knelt down beside him.

"Tricking people out of their money is wrong. It's just like cheating on homework," she told him gently.

Spanky held his head down low. "I'm sorry, Miss Crabtree," he said in a small voice.

"And what are we to do with this money? We can't give it back to all these people, one by one," Miss Crabtree asked.

Suddenly, Spanky had a great idea. He whispered it into Miss Crabtree's ear. Slowly she began to smile. She liked Spanky's idea very much.

* * *

A few minutes later, the curtain rose inside the talent show tent. The first contestants were Waldo and Darla. Waldo was wearing a white tuxedo. Smiling at the audience, he took his seat at the baby grand piano that was on the stage. On top of the piano, wearing a red dress, was Darla. Behind them, hanging by a rope, was a large, cardboard half-moon.

Waldo began to play, and together, he and Darla started their song. The duet was beautiful. The audience clapped loudly as the two kids took their bows.

42

Outside, clouds of dust formed behind The Blur as Alfalfa and Petey sped up at the tent. They had arrived just as Waldo and Darla were finishing their song.

"Miss Crabtree, you just gotta let me sing!" Alfalfa pleaded. Miss Crabtree looked down at him. In her hand was a clipboard with a list of all the acts in the show.

"I'm sorry, Alfalfa," she said, looking at her list. "We're very tightly booked."

Alfalfa put a sad face on. "But my great-great-great aunt flew in from Vulgaria and she's knocking on Death's door and her last wish is to hear me croon and—"

Miss Crabtree put her hand on Alfalfa's shoulder. She saw how much this meant to him. "I love the way your mind works," she said with a laugh. "I think we can squeeze you in."

Alfalfa threw his arms around the teacher. "Thanks, Miss Crabtree," he said, giving her a big hug.

Just then, Waldo and Darla took their bows and exited the stage. Darla went to the left. But Waldo exited to the right—walking straight into Alfalfa.

"Well, well, if it isn't Falafel," sneered Waldo. As soon as Miss Crabtree had said he could participate, Alfalfa had gone backstage to try to warm up his voice.

"It's Alfalfa," he replied evenly. He took a sip of water.

Waldo shrugged. "Whatever. I hope you didn't miss my duet with Darla. It was stupendous. She wasn't bad, either."

But Alfalfa didn't listen. Trying to ignore him, he began to practice again. "I'm the barber of Seville," he sang, belting out the words like an opera star. He turned to Waldo. "I'm about to win Darla back through song."

"Darla? She detests you!" Waldo said meanly.

Alfalfa smiled knowingly. "Not after I serenade her. Darla can't resist my voice. She said so herself," he informed

Waldo.

In only a few moments, Alfalfa would be taking the stage. He cleared his throat, closed his eyes, and began to practice.

Suddenly Waldo had an idea. He grabbed a bottle of liquid soap that was sitting on a shelf. Quickly, he pumped a huge glob into Alfalfa's water glass. There! That would fix him. But before Alfalfa took a sip, Miss Crabtree ushered him out on stage. His plan foiled, Waldo folded his arms, and went out to watch the show with Darla.

In the very last row of the auditorium sat the Rascals. Spanky gathered everyone around. "Well, fellas," he said eagerly, "I convinced Miss Crabtree to take the money we collected and use it as first prize in the Go-Cart Derby!"

The boys were thrilled. "Just think," Stymie said, dollar signs in his eyes, "in three days the money's ours!"

Froggy nodded excitedly. "Everything else may have gone wrong but there's no way we can lose the race."

The boys got up to leave. At that moment, the curtain rose on the stage—and there was Alfalfa! The Rascals stopped in their tracks. Darla covered her eyes.

"This is a song about a tragic romance," began Alfalfa. "I fell in love with a girl, and through schemes and betrayals by my best friend ..."

Spanky's eyes grew wide. Alfalfa had found out about the sabotage plan!

"... the girl fell out of love with me," continued Alfalfa. "She thought I was nothing more than a he-man woman-hater. But I am something more. I'm a woman lover!" he said full of confidence.

The Rascals were furious. They watched as Alfalfa lifted a glass to toast Darla. It was the glass that was filled with soap!

Darla scrunched down in her seat. If Alfalfa didn't say her

name, no one would know it was her. But it was not to be.

"To Darla!" declared Alfalfa, taking a big sip of the soapy drink. Waldo broke out into a big grin. His trick would work!

Chapter 12

Best Buddies

Alfalfa's face grew red. Frowning, he tried to swallow the soapy water. He turned to the orchestra that was behind them and gave them a signal to start.

As he opened his lips for the first verse, a large bubble came out of his mouth! The bubble distracted Alfalfa for a moment. But he continued. As he sang, more bubbles came out of his mouth. They didn't stop Alfalfa.

Soon more bubbles floated across the auditorium. Two of them landed on a surprised Miss Crabtree! Darla was horrified. She covered her face with her hands. The Rascals weren't happy, either.

"I'm gonna put that fool out of our misery!" Spanky whispered loudly. He slid out of his seat and raced backstage.

Still Alfalfa sang on. His shrill voice echoed throughout the room.

Spanky arrived backstage. If he could just find the right rope to pull the curtain down. He looked at the several ropes that hung from the ceiling and picked one.

But that rope didn't work the curtain. It made the cardboard half-moon move. Down, down, down went the moon. Alfalfa didn't notice a thing. He was too wrapped up in his song. Until the corner of the moon snagged the back of his suspenders.

Alfalfa's eyes grew wide. As Spanky pulled the other end of the rope, the moon began to go back up. And Alfalfa went up with it!

Higher and higher went the moon. And higher and higher went Alfalfa. "This may be the King Wedgie of all time!" whispered Froggy, pointing to Alfalfa's pants. The waistband almost reached the back of his neck!

While Alfalfa had been singing, Porky and Buckwheat had sneaked out of the tent. They returned with ripe, juicy tomatoes. Quickly, they passed them out to the other Rascals.

SPLAT! A tomato hit Alfalfa squarely in the face. *WHAM! SPLAT!* Tomato after tomato hit their target. Right then, Alfalfa's suspenders unhooked. With a thump, he fell to the stage floor.

Jumping to his feet, he finished his song. Tomato juice ran down his face. With a look of hope in his eyes, he turned to face Darla.

But she didn't want to see him. "Alfalfa, I hate you!" she cried. The embarrassed girl got up and ran from the tent. Alfalfa was right behind her.

Before he knew what he was saying, Alfalfa blurted out, "But you said at the ballet recital that you loved my singing!"

Darla took a step backward. "Wait a second. That was you at the ballet? You … you … you spy in a tutu!"

At that moment, Waldo strolled out of the tent. "Nice act, you twit," he sneered. "At the go-cart race, it will be my pleasure to precipitate your final degradation."

Alfalfa didn't understand Waldo's fancy words. "You're gonna be in the race?" he asked.

Waldo nodded. "I don't know which I shall enjoy more— my winning or your losing." He took Darla's hand, and the two kids walked off.

As Alfalfa watched them go, the Rascals came running out of the tent.

"Well, hello, Mr. Bubbles," giggled Froggy.

Spanky was very angry. "That was the most disgusting display of she-man woman-loving I've ever seen!"

"Don't talk to me, you Benedict Arnold! This is all your fault!" shouted Alfalfa. The two boys continued to argue. Until Spanky realized something. If Alfalfa was with them … who was watching The Blur?

The boys raced to the other side of the tent. Gone. The Blur was gone!

Porky sniffled. Froggy looked close to tears. The Blur was the Rascals' pride and joy. Without it, they couldn't enter the Derby—and win the money to rebuild their clubhouse.

Spanky spun around. "That's it!" he screamed at Alfalfa. "What's worst of all is I don't even have a club to throw you out of!"

Alfalfa glared back at his friend-turned-enemy. "Well, you sewage-swigging slimeball, if there still was a club, I'd quit!" He stormed off.

The next day wasn't much fun for the Rascals. Without their club—and without each other—there wasn't much worth doing. Everyone felt bad about the words that had been exchanged. Especially Alfalfa and Spanky.

Baseball in hand, Stymie headed over to Alfalfa's house. "Why doncha go make up with him, Alfalfa?" he suggested. "You guys've been friends since you were one."

Alfalfa pouted. "He started it," he said stubbornly.

Stymie tossed his ball in his glove. "And you should finish it. You're a team. Like Bert and Ernie. Superman and

Clark Kent. Beans and wienies." He looked over at Alfalfa. This wouldn't be easy.

A few minutes later, Stymie had arrived at Spanky's house. Stymie told him the same thing he'd told Alfalfa. "At least go talk to him. You only make a once-in-a-lifetime buddy once in a lifetime."

Spanky put his head in his hands. Maybe Stymie was right. He had to admit, he'd been pretty mean. It would be a nice gesture to apologize. He'd show he was the bigger man.

Getting up from his porch, he trudged over to Alfalfa's. He counted each crack in the sidewalk as he walked. He was so busy counting, he didn't notice when someone passed him on the other side of the street. That someone was Alfalfa!

Alfalfa had also decided to apologize. But he didn't notice Spanky walking past, either. He rang Spanky's doorbell. To his dismay, Spanky's dad told him Spanky wasn't there.

When Spanky rang Alfalfa's doorbell, Alfalfa's mom answered. She told him that Alfalfa wasn't home.

Both boys had the same thought. They both thought that the other didn't want to talk. Each boy walked down to the clubhouse.

"Alfalfa!" said Spanky when he saw him.

"Spanky!" said Alfalfa. They looked at the ruined clubhouse.

Nervously, Alfalfa touched his cowlick. "I'm sorry I called you a sewage-swigging slimeball," he said quietly.

Spanky shifted his feet. "I'm sorry I called you names," he admitted.

"I'm sorry I called you a barf-encrusted jumbo-jerk," Alfalfa went on.

Spanky gave him a funny look. "You *didn't* call me a barf-encrusted jumbo-jerk," he said, annoyed.

"Oh. Well, I guess I was just thinking about it," Alfalfa told him. "And I'm sorry about the fire."

Spanky forgave him. After all, he was sorry too. He had tried to mess up Alfalfa's romantic lunch with Darla. Maybe he was a bit responsible for the fire, too.

The two boys walked around the clubhouse. "You know, Spanky," confided Alfalfa, "I like girls. It might even get worse as I get older. Couldn't we be a club because we *like* something?"

Spanky sighed. He wanted to make his best friend happy. But rules were rules. "Without a clubhouse, we don't have a club," he answered dejectedly.

From behind a tree appeared Stymie. "You guys burned down a clubhouse, not a club," he said.

And from the bushes came the voices of Froggy and Uh-Huh. "A club is buddies who stick together, no matter what!" they said in unison.

Porky and Buckwheat popped up from behind a rock pile. "A club is us!" they shouted.

The Rascals all looked at one another. So what if they didn't have a clubhouse? They had each other! Spanky and Alfalfa grinned. And then the two boys shook hands. They were best friends once more. Everyone cheered.

"I just wish we could enter the Go-Cart Derby," said Alfalfa sadly. "But it's impossible."

Spanky clapped his hands. "Who says it's impossible?" he asked the Rascals. "Every one of us, working together, doing whatever it takes to build the best darn go-cart this town has ever seen—that's all the possible we need!" he said, his voice brimming with confidence.

Everyone cheered again. They couldn't wait to get started. There was a lot of work to do.

Chapter 13

Derby Day

Before they could start to build a new go-cart, the Rascals had to put their thoughts down on paper. First, everyone met at Alfalfa's house. Stymie, Alfalfa, and Spanky sketched their ideas on construction paper. No one liked the first idea. Or the second. But the third had definite possibilities.

Spanky gathered the Rascals around him. In order to carry out their plan, they'd need to get lots of materials. Each Rascal would be responsible for getting something for the go-cart.

Stymie borrowed his baby brother's highchair. Spanky and Alfalfa took parts of Spanky's washing machine. Together, Buckwheat, Porky, and Uh-Huh contributed a trash can. One Rascal after the other came running back to Alfalfa's backyard, with things they could use for the go-cart.

As fast as they could, the boys worked on building a new go-cart. Piece by piece, it began to take shape. Finally, the boys were finished. With excitement in their faces, they stepped back to admire their work. Some people might have thought it was a pile of junk. But the Rascals were proud. They had joined together ... and had become a club again.

Alfalfa handed Spanky a can of soda.

"I christen thee, The Blur II: The Sequel," Spanky proclaimed, hitting the new go-cart with the can. Soda spurted out of the can, and shot into the air.

"Yeah!" yelled the boys.

Spanky took out a set of keys, and handed them to Alfalfa. "Do us proud, buddy," he told him warmly. Grinning, Alfalfa accepted the keys. The Rascals crowded around him, patting him on the back. And then they all took out soda cans—and poured them over Alfalfa, themselves, and The Blur II. It was time to celebrate!

*   *   *

Finally, the big day had come. The county fair was jam packed. Hundreds of people were waiting at the starting line. And just as many people were waiting at the finishing line. Even the mayor was there to watch the race.

The race announcer stepped up to the podium, and picked up a microphone. "Ladies and gentlemen, boys and girls, welcome to the Seventy-Third Annual Go-Cart Derby!" she said.

Alfalfa and Spanky stood by The Blur II, their hearts pounding. They put on their helmets and climbed into the go-cart.

The race announcer told the crowd where the race would start and finish. All of the Rascals listened carefully. Except for Buckwheat and Porky. They were late.

As the two boys hurried to the starting line, they passed a sign with a large arrow painted on it. Porky gave the arrow a playful spin, and continued on his way. He didn't realize that the arrow showed the way to the final turn of the race!

"The first racer across the finish line will receive this genuine gold-plated cubic zirconium trophy," the announcer said. "And—a prize of five hundred dollars!"

52

She held up a nickle jar filled with money. "Let's hear it for these fine young men!"

The crowd applauded loudly.

Alfalfa and Spanky looked over the competition. There were eight other go-carts in the race. They spotted a smug-looking Butch in one of them.

"How're we gonna beat that?" asked Alfalfa. He looked at it carefully. It looked just like The Blur!

"...aaay ..." said the boys slowly. It was the Blur! Butch and Woim had stolen it! But there wasn't time to do anything now. The race was about to begin.

Just then, a tenth racer pulled up to the starting line. The racer had shiny metal and sleek lines. The turbo engine hummed. Everyone oohed and ahhed.

Inside the racer were Darla and Waldo. Each wore a silver helmet. Darla had her helmet visor down over her face.

Alfalfa and Spanky were pretty nervous. They did not know how The Blur II would handle against this racer. But Alfalfa had an idea. He took out Darla's handkerchief, and tied it onto the hood ornament.

"All great knights ride into battle wearing the colors of their lady," he told Spanky. Spanky rolled his eyes. Darla sat up in her seat. That was a pretty nice gesture, she admitted to herself. Waldo frowned, and put his helmet visor down.

At that moment, a green flag rose and fell. The race was on! Waldo's racer sped ahead of everyone. Butch and Woim were close behind. Laughing evilly, they pushed a button. Gooey string shot out from the rear bumper. Trying to avoid the string, three racers crashed into bushes.

As they neared the second turn, Alfalfa stepped on the gas pedal. Soon, they were right next to Waldo and Darla, and Butch and Woim.

"You stole our racer!" Spanky yelled angrily.

Butch gave Spanky a dirty look. "Finders keepers, losers suck," he told him. Each racer sped on.

They neared the final turn. Alfalfa and then Butch went straight—the way the arrow pointed. It was the same arrow Porky had turned to indicate the wrong way!

"Waldo, I think we're supposed to turn here," said Darla worriedly when they came to the arrow. But Waldo shook his head. He followed Alfalfa and Butch.

Within a few seconds, a race official hurried over to the arrow. He put it back so it pointed the right way. He didn't realize that three racers had already missed the turn.

Alfalfa and Spanky, Butch and Woim, Waldo and Darla— all three go-carts came flying into the center of the city. People screamed, and tried to get out of the way. The go-carts turned, and headed down an empty road.

Waldo didn't care if people got hurt. He just wanted to win. "It's time to lose these losers," he told Darla. He turned a knob, and his racer picked up speed.

"They're getting away!" cried Spanky. In desperation, Alfalfa looked down at the dials. REGULAR WASH. HEAVY LOAD. SPIN CYCLE. It was the panel from Spanky's washing machine. Spin cycle, he decided and pushed the button. The Blur II began to spin—and then shot forward.

Not to be left behind, Butch and Woim activated their rocket boosters. There was just one problem. They'd put the rockets in reverse. Their racer sped off—*backwards!*

Chapter 14

Two Big Surprises

Now Waldo and Alfalfa were in the lead. Waldo smiled. This would be easy. He flicked a button and blades popped out from his wheels.

"Yikes! Spikes!" shrieked Alfalfa, trying to dodge the blades. It was no use. The Blur II spun out of control and headed into a busy street.

"Don't panic, don't panic," cried Spanky, gripping the side of the racer. Cars swerved out of the way. Alfalfa kept his eyes on the road.

Waldo and Darla were now in the lead. Darla was very upset.

"You scuzz bucket!" she said to Waldo. "You could've hurt them!"

"Oh please. Don't trouble yourself about that liquid-soap-swilling bubble-spouting nincompoop!" he said, irritated. Darla's eyes grew wide and she nodded to herself. It all made sense now.

"So you're responsible for the bubbles at the talent show!" she said accusingly. "Pull over!"

Waldo slammed on the brakes. "You're getting to be a real pain in the gluteus maximus," he said and pulled over. A few minutes later, with only one person inside, the racer sped off down the road again.

Somehow, someway, everyone found their way back to the real course. They sped down the track, with Waldo's racer in the lead. Butch's racer was in second. And Alfalfa's was in third. In the distance were four other racers.

Butch turned his head. There was no way that Alfalfa and Spanky were going to beat him. He pulled out a huge flare. *BANG!* He tossed it back, where it landed on The Blur II's hood ... and right on Darla's handkerchief.

Smoke poured out of the flare, blinding Alfalfa and Spanky.

"I can't see!" screamed Alfalfa.

Just then, Waldo pulled up. He took out a fire extinguisher and put the burning flare out. With a wave, Waldo raced ahead. Spanky was shocked.

"What a guy!" he said. He couldn't believe the rich boy had actually done something nice.

VROOM! The racers headed toward the finish line. Waldo was in the lead. Then Butch. And then Alfalfa. It was going to be a close one. Excitedly, the crowd leapt to their feet. They cheered the racers on. The Rascals called out words of encouragement to Alfalfa and Spanky.

Just then, the handkerchief flew off the hood ornament. It hit Alfalfa squarely in the face. With a look of determination in his eyes, Alfalfa started to climb out of the driver's seat.

"Grab the wheel!" he instructed Spanky.

Spanky was horrified. "This is no time for hanky panky!" said Spanky. "We got a finish line to cross!"

Alfalfa shook his head. "Not without this," he told him, holding up the handkerchief. As Spanky took the wheel, Alfalfa climbed carefully onto the hood of the racer. He bent down and began to tie it.

The crowd screamed louder. Butch gritted his teeth, and pushed on his pedal. Waldo leaned forward in determination. Spanky, his eyes half shut in fear, gripped the wheel. And Alfalfa kept trying to tie the handkerchief.

Whoosh! A checkered flag was raised and brought down. The race was over. And ... Alfalfa's cowlick had crossed the finish line first! The Blur II had won by a hair! The prize money was theirs!

As The Blur II came to a stop next to the livestock show, the Rascals went wild. They raced down to the finish line.

"You did it, Alfalfa! You won!" shouted Buckwheat.

Alfalfa clutched Darla's handkerchief in his sweaty hand. "No. *We* did it. All of us!" he replied. Everyone cheered. "And to think we won because of this, the symbol of my amour!" Alfalfa said triumphantly, holding up the hankie.

Butch and Woim had climbed out of their racer. They stormed over to the Rascals. "It ain't right," Butch told them angrily. "We go to all the trouble of stealing your racer, and you still win!" Butch drew back his fist.

"I'm usually a lover, not a fighter," Alfalfa answered. "But in your case, I'm willing to make an exception." He too drew back his fist. *BAM!* Alfalfa hit Butch smack in the face, knocking him into a pigpen. Woim looked at Alfalfa. He could see Alfalfa meant business. Closing his eyes, Woim dove into the mud next to Butch.

"Nice left, pal!" Spanky said to Alfalfa.

"Gentlemen, let's honor Alfalfa with a 'spoley-oley.' "

The Rascals nodded. "Spoley-oley, spoley-oley, spoley-oley!" they chanted.

Alfalfa was touched. His friends were so great. Just then, he spotted Waldo. "He turned out to be pretty okay," Alfalfa said to the boys.

Spanky ran over to Waldo's racer. This guy deserved some

credit—he'd helped them win. Spanky grabbed the boy's hand began to pump it up and down. "Put it there, pal! You're quite a guy. I understand you're new in town. We have a club. The He-Man Woman-Haters," he informed him, smiling.

At first, Alfalfa smiled, too. But then he realized something. Something shocking! He tapped Spanky on the head.

"Alfalfa, I'm extending a membership offer here," Spanky said, annoyed. He didn't want to be interrupted at an important moment such as this.

"That's not Waldo," Alfalfa said. He pointed a few yards away. There, covered with mud and carrying a helmet, was the real Waldo.

The rich boy spotted the Rascals. "You'll be hearing from my lawyers!" he yelled at them. The Rascals weren't worried about him. They were worried about the person they'd *thought* was Waldo.

"Then, who's the guy who saved us?" Spanky wondered out loud. The racer took off the helmet. It was *Darla!*

"Darla!" cried Alfalfa.

"A ... girl?!" said the other Rascals in horror. As Darla gave them all a big smile, Spanky nearly fainted.

* * *

At the award ceremony, the boys couldn't believe it. Saved by a girl!

"And now it is my great privilege to present the trophy and the prize money to our winners—Alfalfa Switzer and Spanky McFarland!" declared the race announcer.

The crowd clapped loudly. Alfalfa proudly shook the announcer's hand. But something was wrong with Spanky. And Alfalfa knew exactly what it was.

"Don't take it personal, lady. But my pal is real disap-

58

pointed," Alfalfa whispered.

The announcer smiled at Spanky. "What's the matter, sugar pie?" she asked him.

"Uh ... he was kinda hopin' to meet A. J. Ferguson," Alfalfa informed her.

"Famed Indy race-car driver," Spanky said importantly. Probably this woman had never even heard of A. J. Ferguson, he thought to himself.

The announcer smiled. "Well, today's your lucky day, boys, because you just did!" She unzipped her jacket. Underneath was a flashy race-car driver's uniform. The letters on it read A. J. FERGUSON.

Spanky gasped. Another girl! Too stunned to move, he stood stock still while A. J. handed him the trophy, and gave him the jar of money. Then she bent down and gave him a big kiss on the cheek.

The Rascals held their breath. What would the president of the He-Man Woman-Haters' Club do now?

"Let's even things up," Spanky said blushing. "How 'bout one on this side?" he asked her, turning his cheek. Laughing, A. J. gave Spanky another kiss.

Chapter 15

Everything's A-O-kay!

This had been some day for the Rascals. One they'd never forget. After the awards ceremony, they all joined together to walk home. Spanky held the trophy in his arms.

A few feet behind everyone else was Alfalfa with Darla and Mary Ann.

"I saw what you did, Alfalfa. With my handkerchief. That was very heartwarming," Darla told him kindly.

Mary Ann gripped her hands together. "And awfully romantical," she sighed.

Alfalfa didn't know quite what to say. "Gee, thanks. But … I thought you hated me," he confided.

Darla shook her head emphatically. "I don't hate you. It's just that sometimes you do mean things. Like playing tricks on me at our picnic," she said.

Her words carried through the air … straight to Spanky's ears. He turned. "Uh … I can explain that," he said. "It was me who wrecked your picnic with Alfalfa. I thought you were spinning your womanly web to snare my pal. But I was the one who sabotaged you and Alfalfa behind your backs. I guess I was the web spinner," he confessed.

Alfalfa and Darla looked at each other. Now Darla knew that Alfalfa really *did* like her. And Alfalfa knew that Darla didn't care about Waldo—she cared about *him!*

"My Alfalfinator!" cried Darla.

"My delectable Darlooney!" sighed Alfalfa. Just like he did during their picnic in the clubhouse, he wiggled his eyebrows and ears. Then Darla did what she'd done that day. She stuck out her tongue and touched her nose.

Ahhh. True love. As the Rascals smiled their approval, Alfalfa and Darla gave each other a very big hug.

*　*　*

A few weeks later, things were pretty much back to normal. The Rascals had used the money Alfalfa and Spanky had won in the race to buy wood. They had worked hard over the last fourteen days. Chopping and sawing and hammering, they had put back their old clubhouse piece by piece.

The trophy the boys had won sat on a special new shelf. And they'd gotten The Blur back from Butch and Woim. Next to it, the Rascals had parked The Blur II.

The new clubhouse looked exactly like the old clubhouse. But there was one thing that was different now. All of the Rascals were there for a meeting. And on a bench next to Alfalfa sat Darla. On his other side was Mary Ann.

"Shocking! Unbelievable!" Froggy said.

"Stupidifying!" chimed in Mary Ann. She gave Spanky a dreamy-eyed look.

"Uh-huh," put in Uh-Huh.

After all this time, the Rascals had decided to let girls in the club. It had been a landslide vote. Even Spanky had voted yes.

Stymie stood. "You know, it would be boring if we were all exactly alike," he admitted. "When you get right down to it, boys and girls are the same where it matters, and different where it counts."

"Uh-huh," said Uh-Huh. He agreed with that.

Spanky wanted to voice his opinion. "Have we betrayed our forefathers? Have we trampled on all the honest woman-haters who came before us—"

Darla interrupted him. "Or is he just being a total and complete idiot?" she asked.

"Uh-huh," said Uh-Huh again. ignored Darla. "You're having second thoughts, too, aren't you, Uh-Huh?"

Uh-Huh shook his head no. "Uh-uh," he said.

Everyone turned to look at Uh-Huh.

"Uh-Huh learned a new word!" yelled Stymie. Even Petey, the dog, was surprised.

"Actually, I've always had rather an extensive vocabulary, not to mention a phenomenal grasp of grammar and a superlative command of syntax," Uh-Huh told the boys. "I've simply chosen not to employ them," he finished.

Laughing, Alfalfa and Darla looked at each other. Despite the bad things, they had had a lot of fun lately. And now the Rascals had even changed their motto—HE-MAN WOMAN-HATERS' CLUB. WOMEN WELCOME.